A PRESENT FOR SANTA

Written and Illustrated by John Patience

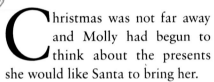

Christmas was not far away and Molly had begun to think about the presents she would like Santa to bring her.

"A paint box, a computer game, a pair of roller blades."

Then suddenly she had a strange idea.

"Santa brings everyone presents, doesn't he, Pickles?" she said to her cuddly rabbit. "But what does Santa get for Christmas? Nothing at all. Well I'm going to get him a present."

So that's what Molly did. She bought a present for Santa and wrapped it herself in Christmas wrapping paper.

That night Molly wrote Santa a letter:

Dear Santa,
I have bought you a
Christmas present.
Can I come to your Grotto
and give it to you?
Love from Molly.

Molly opened her bedroom window and threw the letter out into the air. It was caught by the North Wind. He carried it far, far away to Santa in his Grotto at the North Pole.

At last it was Christmas Eve and Molly had almost forgotten about her letter to Santa. She was climbing into bed when she heard tapping on her windowpane. She opened it and in blew the North Wind.

"Santa has invited you to visit him in his grotto," he blustered. "I am to take you there. It's very cold out so you'd better put on your dressing gown,"

Molly did as the North Wind suggested. She picked up her present for Santa and Pickles, her cuddly rabbit, climbed onto the North Wind's back and off they flew!

The North Wind carried Molly away and away, high over the snowy rooftops, over the fields and the deep, dark ocean to the sparkling, frozen land of the North Pole.

"What are those beautiful, coloured lights in the sky?" asked Molly.

"They are the Northern Lights," said the North Wind. "And look down there. That's Santa's Grotto."

Molly looked down and saw something like a fairy tale castle but entirely made of ice. Molly was so surprised that she almost dropped Pickles. That would have spoiled everything.

Santa was waiting at the door to welcome Molly, who handed him her present.

"Thank you very much," he said. "Do you know, no-one has ever given me a Christmas present before!"

Santa showed Molly around his workshop. His helpers were still busy making toys.

"We've almost finished now," said Santa. "Just one or two wooden trains, a few rocking horses to paint, some cuddly toys to finish off and then we'll be ready to go."

"It must be very hard work," said Molly.

"Oh, it is!" chuckled Santa. "I've been on my feet all day and these boots are killing me!"

Molly looked at Santa's boots and smiled a secret, little smile.

Soon the last toy was finished and it was time to load up the sleigh.

"Would you like to help, Molly? Asked Santa.

"Oh, yes please!" replied Molly. "Can Pickles help too?"

"I should think so," said Santa.

Then he took a jar labelled Fairy Dust down from the shelf and sprinkled a little over the little, pink rabbit. Immediately it came to life!

With everyone lending a hand the sleigh was loaded in next to no time.

Molly had great fun helping Santa to deliver the presents, popping them down the chimneys but, by the time the job was finished, it was very late and Molly and Pickles were very tired. They both fell fast asleep beside Santa on the sleigh. When he arrived at Molly's house, Santa climbed through the open window and popped Molly and Pickles, still sleeping, into bed. He took Molly's presents from his bag and laid them at the foot of the bed.

"Merry Christmas," he whispered.

Santa returned to the North Pole on his sleigh and arrived just as the sun was rising. It was Christmas morning.

Time to open my present from Molly," said Santa.

He tore off the wrapping paper and opened the cardboard box. It was a pair of slippers with a little reindeer on each toe. They fitted perfectly.

"Just what I needed!" laughed Santa, doing a jolly dance to show them off. "Ho, ho, ho!"